Among
The
Aspen

Among The Aspen

Latent Origin

WILLIAM ATES

Special thanks extended to:
Front and back cover photos courtesy of S. Roshaven
Encouragement and criterial input Raymond 'Bob" Whritenour

Book design by Maureen Cutajar
www.gopublished.com

ISBN: 978-0-692-55724-2

In loving memory

S.J.W.

Made a world where memories flourished

Author's Note

The story you are about to read and become part of is based entirely on true-life events. However, industry standard dictates that it must be categorized as fiction for the following reason: To protect and preserve, I (The Author) have changed the name of places where the events had taken place. Those who enjoy camping, hiking, fishing or any other recreational outdoor activities at their favorite locations will especially understand my reasons for such changes.

BASED ON TRUE EVENTS

If there is no vision when standing in an open field, close the eyes and begin to see again.

— WIBIL

Chapter I

I am returned. From where can not be easily said. The mind is idle and without formulation of thought. The struggle of body to continue is the sole working function. The human senses do not exist. I am only able to recognize that a small amount of light is penetrating my closed eyelids. I am trapped in a place so few may attempt to describe. I am caught somewhere between that which lives and that which does not. With the same quickness that returned me I am gone.

I am again within myself. For the second time I am able to recognize a small amount of light penetrating my closed eyelids. However, this return seems to be different than the last. I can now feel and understand that I am lying flat on my back. I remain motionless caught in a place where time refuses to be measured. I struggle and can barely open my eyes. This simple bodily action that I had never given any thought about previously was now a difficult task to perform.

My eyes begin slowly focusing as I continue to force them open. I could now see that the sunlight was penetrating through a piece of fabric. The filtering of the sunlight through the fabric turned it a bluish hue. I stared at the fabric overhead without trying to move. For how long I could not say. I began to feel an increase of recognition slowly returning to me. I moved my legs slightly one at a time and then my arms. There was a stiff and numb like feeling in them. I did not know if I was capable of feeling pain but none was felt. Tired, I was very tired. A feeling of exhaustion overwhelmed both my mind and body. I bent my right knee slightly pulling my leg toward my head. I pulled my left arm over and across my body allowing me to roll onto my right side. Now lying on the right side of my face, I brought both hands up to cover it. I closed my eyes and went to sleep.

I opened my eyes to exit what could only be described as a deep coma like sleep. For many minutes I laid there on my right side with both hands still shielding my face. One instinctual thought began to motivate me. I had to try and move. I had to try and move and at least sit up. With less effort than before I moved my hands away from my face. I rolled to my left and was again lying on my back. I bent my knees and pulled my legs toward my body so that my feet were flat on the ground about two feet apart and a few inches from my rear. I placed both hands over my face and began rubbing gently up and down as one would do if they were washing with soap and water.

Several seconds later I put my arms down to my sides and began focusing on the surroundings.

Moving only my eyes I began to recognize the color and design of the fabric. I was lying inside of a tent. I turned my head to the left and saw a backpack in the corner of the tent. All of the contents had been removed and were strewn chaotically around the corner and left side of the tent. Using my elbows for leverage I forced myself to sit up. An immediate dizziness overcame me. I moved no further and sat staring down and forward to regain focus. After a minute or so I brought my hands up elbows on thighs and covered my face with them. Slowly the dizzy feeling faded as I sat there.

I lowered my hands into my lap. I had regained enough focus to resume an inspection of my surroundings. A sleeping bag was stretched out like a blanket beneath me. I was fully clothed including shoes on my feet. The fabric was drawn and tied shut over the window opening on the side of the tent. Both the fabric and inner screen doors of the tent were zipped closed from the inside.

Questions began entering my mind as I sat slumped forward so as not to fall backward. What happened? What caused this condition I was in? How long have I been here? How long was I asleep? Still disoriented I had no answers to ease the thoughts of this moment. Every muscle felt stiff and ached slightly when I used them to perform the most basic movements of my body.

For several more minutes I moved and inspected both my hands checking the function and dexterity. I scooted forward on my rear toward the tent and proceeded to unzip both the screen and fabric doors. I felt a cramp-like pain in my right calf that eased a bit when I straightened the leg. I opened the screen and fabric doors of the tent. The unfiltered sunlight immediately poured into the tent through the opening. The brighter light forced a harsh squint onto my face as my eyes tried to compensate the change in illumination. While my eyes adjusted I managed to tie the door flaps to the side so they remained open. The air outside was warm and nourishing compared to the stale heaviness that lingered within the tent.

From my seated position I began to survey the area outside the tent that was visible through the door opening. The view was limited and I saw only the mountainous terrain of the campsite. It was very quiet outside. The only sound I heard was a light breeze moving the swaying tree limbs and bushes. Placing my palms on the ground to help lift my weight I scooted backward on my rear into the tent.

I sat in the middle of the tent and only a few moments later a memory started to replay in my mind.

Chapter II

I wanted to get an early start and enjoy as much of the holiday weekend as I could. I finished loading my camping and fishing gear into the truck and left home around five in the morning. The drive time to the campsite was about four hours. From previous experiences I knew that the area was a popular destination for many sportsman and outdoor enthusiasts. If I did not get there early the best campsites would be taken and the campground may be full leaving no spots available. I arrived at the entrance to the campground just before nine in the morning.

At the entrance into the campground there was a wooden sign about forty by eighteen with writing etched into it. It read – Trikumwith Water Canyon – and below the name was – overnight camping $2 per night. Between the two etched lines a narrow slot was cut in the center face of the sign for a camper to deposit the money into a collection box mounted on the back. The campground operated on an honor system. There was no park attendant on duty to collect the money nor could I remember there ever being one whenever I visited previously. I put the truck in park, walked to the sign, and stuffed five folded $1 bills into the slot. I got back into the truck and entered the camp-ground.

With only a few bends the dirt road led gently into the canyon about one and a half miles and ended in a circular turnaround a little over two hundred and twelve feet wide. Nestled between steep parallel mountain slopes that rose about one hundred sixty-six feet high the basin of the canyon was about one third of a mile in width.

Trikum Creek wound widely through the canyon hugging the base of a steep slope in one area and then swept across to the other steeply sloped side of the canyon the entire length of the road. The creek was seventeen to eighteen feet wide with an average depth of a foot and a half. Natural stones both rounded and jagged exposed by the erosive flow of water lined the creek bed. There were many locations where one could cross the creek by stepping across the tops of the stones if inclined to do so.

Narrow single lane bridges were erected along the roadway allowing the creek to cross sides a total of four times. The winding of the creek and placement of the dirt road created large flat areas throughout the canyon basin. Repeated use by campers had removed most of the head high wild growing brush over the years leaving the open areas now covered with short native grasses. Large pines many decades old with an occasional Cottonwood or Poplar tree flourish sporadically around the canyon floor. A mixture of Bearberry, Crested wheat, Prickly ear and Sage are but a few of the many species of native plants covering the areas less traveled by foot. The large grassy areas make excellent camping sites on either side of the road.

I was not surprised to see the campground already full of visitors as I continued down the stretch of road. Almost all the campsites were already taken as I neared the circular turnaround at the end of the road.

There was only one campsite set up to the left of the circle so I selected a spot on the right side end near the creek. The creek curved left from the right behind the turnaround circle and disappeared into the mountains shortly after. At this campsite the water would be on my right and behind me providing some privacy on two sides should the area fill with visitors later in the day.

I backed the truck in and began unpacking my gear. After selecting a location up-wind fifteen feet from a makeshift stone circle fire pit, I cleared the ground and erected the tent. I put my backpack inside the tent at the far corner and rolled out the sleeping bag. I collected and stacked a dozen more stones around the fire pit to fortify it. Kindling then a couple split logs I brought with me prepared the fire to be lit later at dusk.

Satisfied with the campsite I sat down in a folding chair near the fire pit and began to eat the brown bag lunch I had packed the night before. For now, ham and cheese with chips and a soda was the menu.

Chapter III

I lifted my head and began looking out the tent door opening. My mind was again idle and without thought. I sat paralyzed in the middle of the tent gazing outside for many minutes. Slowly I began to notice the shadow angle of the trees cast by the sunlight on the ground. Based on their position I deduced it to be mid afternoon. I looked down turning my arm to check my watch and it was not on my wrist. I did however notice a couple scratches on my forearm. I must have taken the watch off and it was likely among the items strewn about the tent. I turned to my left and got up on my hands and knees to search for the watch. Almost instantly dizziness overcame me accompanied with a feeling of nausea and a cramp like pain returning in my right calf. I found the watch and returned to a sitting position to straighten my leg and ease the cramp pain. With difficulty I read the watch. It was a little after three in the afternoon.

I returned to a position of lying flat on my back. With both hands over my head I managed to gather enough of the sleeping bag to create a small pillow on which I could prop my head. If I remained still perhaps the dizziness and uneasy feeling in my stomach would pass shortly. After several minutes I felt better and the memory began again.

Chapter IV

After lunch I planned on spending the remainder of the day fishing. From previous trips I knew that the best fishing experience would be further up into the mountains away from the recreation areas. With my fly pole and gear I headed toward the creek from my campsite. There was a path made by the trampling of vegetation no more than a foot wide that followed the creek along the bank. Animals such as deer, bear, coyote, and a few humans were the most likely reason the path existed. It did not take long for me to leave the camping area behind and disappear into the mountains.

Several hundred yards up the path I hiked by a man standing in the creek casting a pole himself. There was a brief exchange of pleasantries as I continued to travel further into the mountains along the water. A few hundred yards later I came upon a stretch of the creek that looked favorable for fishing. Standing on the path I could see no human presence in either direction of the waterway. I prepared myself and entered the creek to begin doing what it was I traveled here to do.

It did not take long for the fish to start jumping at the fly lure. In a span of thirty minutes I had already caught three fish. The catch was two Brook and one Rainbow trout. The three fell short of keep length so I practiced catch and release with all. I decided to leave and try even further up into the mountains. I made my way to the creek bank and slipped while stepping out. The whole of my weight was now on one knee right in the middle of a sage bush. I could feel the short rigid branches of the bush stabbing at my leg through my pants. I regained myself and was again standing on the path. I packed the gear brushed off my pant leg and headed further up the gulch to find another enticing spot.

I surveyed the water from the bank for another potential spot in which to cast a fly while traveling along the path. I had now reached a point of the gulch where the land opened wider away from the sides of the creek. At the mouth of the gulch the span across was around fifty feet and here it was more than seven hundred feet wide. The open flat area allowed for me to see the water further up-stream.

The creek bent to the left a distance then right as it went further into the mountains. Continuing the hike, I had quickly approached the first bend in the creek. Here there were several large boulders lining one side of the path. At this point I estimated to have put a distance of two miles between myself and the campsite. Both my mouth and throat felt very dry which I attributed to the lengthy trek up the path. I decided to take a rest and remedy my thirst. Sipping the water bottle, I sat upon one of the large stones and enjoyed a panoramic view of the tranquil scenery surrounding me.

The distant mountain folds looked rough and dangerous but when approached they became gentler and more enticing to explore. The sunlight glinted off the surface of the creek as the water gently trickled by. The fields around the creek were lush and green with an occasional patch of brown throughout. One particular species of plant was at full bloom this time of year and little golden flowers dotted the entire landscape. This extraordinary high mountain valley is a well kept secret and I am one of the privileged few to have ever laid eyes upon it. Three tenths of an hour had passed from the time I sat. I collected my things and began on the path again.

In this area the trail had almost disappeared into the grass but was still discernable enough to follow. I went about a quarter mile further and began to see a grove of trees ahead of me in the distance. I started to feel tired, not physically tired, but sleepy tired as in need of a nap. The white bark of the trees in the grove shone brightly in the sunlight against the darker backdrop of the mountains as I approached them. The dry mouth and throat that I had no more than half an hour ago returned and was becoming uncomfortable. The sleepy feeling was increasing and I thought it best to again take some rest. I stopped in the middle of the grove removed my backpack and placed it on the ground in the grass. I removed a water bottle then sat down in front of the pack on the grass and leaned against it like a chair back.

I swirled a small amount of water inside my mouth then spat it out to remove the dryness. Then took a few sips of the water wetting the dryness in my throat. Perhaps a combination of an early start, higher altitude, and the hike was causing the sleepy feeling. I looked at the altimeter on my watch and from my starting point of 7,560ft. I had climbed 354ft. in elevation. Knowing the distance and amount of time required for the return trip to the campsite I decided to not fish anymore that day. Instead I would first rest awhile then scout the creek for the next day before beginning the hike back down to the camp areas. I rested my head back and started nodding off.

Minutes later on the edge of sleep I heard the sound of human voices. I sprang to a sitting position and looked around. I saw no one. There was nobody around. Reassured I leaned back on my pack and closed my eyes. A light afternoon breeze blew by me. Moments later I again heard human voices speaking. I quickly sat up and began to look about more intently. I saw no one around. An awkward and unknown feeling crept deep into me. This was something I had never experienced before. Was I so tired that my mind had tricked me into thinking I was hearing people talk? I had heard and read accounts of how dehydration or exhaustion could affect the mental and physical state of an individual. For many minutes I continued to convince myself that I had scientifically answered any mystical questions. I drank more water as the dryness in my mouth and throat continued. The sleepy feeling was overwhelming so I leaned back and again closed my eyes.

Another afternoon breeze blew around and over me as I rested on the grass in the middle of the Aspen grove. It did not take long before the human voices I heard prior had returned. This time I did not sit up and look around. Instead I surrendered to them remaining still and listening. I could hear many different voice tones talking at the same time. I felt another breeze blow over and past me as I tried to single out and hear just one voice at a time.

The voice of a man was talking to me. He presented and explained ancient wood and stone building practices that have been built upon and reused in every human civilization dating back many thousands of years. Then the origin of units of measure was explained to me. I was told about traverse points between different units of measure and how humans created it to be so. 18mi.=30km. and 1.8deg.fahrenheit = 1deg.centigrade.

The voice of a woman instructed me that the first method used by humans to count time was based on a ninth month pregnancy also known as a gestation cycle. She continued to reveal how the movement of the sun through the sky was used to create a twelve-month calendar year and the four primary compass directions. The four letters used to represent the north, east, west and south directions are n-e-w-s.

The voice of another man explained time saving shortcuts called math formulas and their origins. His voice proceeded to explain and reveal that many Hieroglyphs and Pictoglyphs are not words, they are building instructions. A symbol said to represent the word "rake" is the exact same symbol used for the modern day math formula A= D over R, that is angle= distance divided by radius.

Another voice explained to me that the four acids known as adenine, cytosine, guanine, and thymine are measured and used to determine dna of living organisms. The four acids are created in the human body when the daily eating of proteins are converted through the digestive process. No two people eat or drink exactly the same every day so this process of testing can identify an individual just like a fingerprint. Individual diet is abbreviated as I.D.

The information came rapidly and it kept flowing. It was explained to me that the boiling point of water at sea level is two hundred twelve degrees Fahrenheit and freezes at thirty-two degrees. The difference between is one hundred eighty degrees. The helix design of dna is based on a half circle which is one hundred eighty degrees. The metabolic weight of water is eighteen. Computer generated images created by a human artist is a drawing, not a reality. The stages of water being solid, liquid, and vapor can be abbreviated as s-l-a-v. Almost every scientist attached to the creation and development of what has been labeled dna were from Europe during the eighteenth century.

The voice of an older woman explained the use of plant and earth compounds. The combinations used for tens of thousands of years by humans have multiple applications such as medicines. Many medicines can cause a side effect creating another problem in the body requiring yet another medicine. All medicines made by humans came through trial and error over the course of many thousands of years. Nefarious individuals have also used the mixture of compounds to create poisons. A mixture of compounds can neither be labeled medicinal or poisonous until it has been repeatedly tested on human subjects and the effect documented thereafter. Throughout history many human subjects were both unknowing and unwilling participants in these experiments. One such recent example was the widespread administering of oil extracted from the castor bean. Known and labeled as a poison, ricin also comes from the castor bean. An unknown number of uninformed people worldwide were instructed and gave this compound to their children as medicine. In the lengthy history of humanity only a few individuals have willingly agreed to be test subjects in the name of medical science.

The high mountain wind had transformed itself into a sound that I would hear and comprehend. Simple information that is not taught in a classroom or printed in any book that clearly revealed the origin of how humans create circled squarely in my mind. An immeasurable amount of knowledge that extended deeply into the human past and present had somehow been spoken into me. The feeling of having become a wiser person was inherited by what I know as the Eocene within the wind.

I opened my eyes and saw an enormous bull elk staring pensively at me standing no more than three feet away. I stayed motionless and for tens of seconds the elk and I stared at each other. The poised stance and look in the eyes of the elk was as though he had been guarding over me while I rested and listened to the winds of truth. The elk lowered his massive head and gently pushed at my foot with his nose in a nudging fashion. To my one side a large owl began to take flight, and on my other, a golden eagle also began flying away. Confident that I was now fully awakened the bull elk calmly walked through the grass and then vanished from my site among the Aspen.

Chapter V

My focus narrowed on a small area of stitching where the tent roof met the front wall and the sunlight pierced through more brightly. I felt a cool dampness all the way around my neck and at my waist. I pulled the front of the shirt down away from my neck and saw that it was wet with perspiration. Lifting the bottom, I saw that it too was soaked all the way around. Having seen this, I knew immediately that I had to have been sweating profusely for quite some length of time to drench the shirt in such a manner.

Pushing myself up using my elbows then hands to assist I came to a sitting position. I leaned to my left bracing myself with my hand planted away from my body and began sifting through the items scattered around that side of the tent. After finding what I was looking for, I returned to a centered sitting position. Without hesitating I removed the wet shirt and tossed it to the front of the tent on the right side of the door opening. While pulling the clean dry shirt down over my head and body I again felt the dizziness, nausea, and cramping pain in my calf.

Desire to get to my feet and move around was in my thoughts but my body was now in charge of dictating and restricting what it was I could or could not do. This was a surreal reversal of what I had been accustomed to and taken for granted in all the previous years of my life. I thought it best to sit longer until I felt well enough to attempt getting to my feet. I ran my hand over the sleeping bag on the ground behind me. It too was soaking wet acting like a sponge to catch the perspiration from my body that the shirt could no longer hold. The finding again confirmed that I had been sweating a lot and for a long duration of time.

In addition to the other symptoms there was a hazy somewhat drunken feeling affecting me. With the exception of a couple beers I did not bring alcohol whereby omitting it as a possible cause for this feeling. I was able to recognize how I felt and lethargically perform simple movements but still could not remember the events that led to this present condition of ailment. I sat empty of thought for minutes peering out the tent door until again the memory resumed.

Chapter VI

I waited until after the elk had disappeared from my sight before looking about in other directions around me. From my seated view I saw no movements of any living creature. It was getting later in the afternoon as I stood up in the grass and began preparing my backpack for travel. I started up the path to inspect the creek for the next day of fishing. Upon exiting the grove of trees I saw that the gulch continued wide for some distance. After hiking a couple hundred yards, the creek had moved away from the path about seventy feet to the right. It was becoming harder to see through the brush growing in the flat area between.

I left the path and started through the brush to better see the water. Nearing the creek, I clearly saw a dam of sticks and logs blocking the flow of water creating a pool about thirty feet round behind it. No doubt this is the work of a busy little carpenter. The width of the creek before the dam was only half as wide as it was after the obstruction. I did not want to disturb this area and began following the bank heading upstream.

Only twenty paces along I turned to look back and saw an adult beaver following me. I watched over my shoulder as it continued to follow in a friendly manner while I walked. I decided to play around a little to see what it would do. When I went left it went left, and when I went right it too went right. I allowed it to continue a distance longer then stopped and slowly turned to face the dam builder. When I turned around the beaver stopped about twenty feet behind me. I spoke in a soft polite tone urging the beaver to return home and gave reassurance that I would be fine continuing on my own. The beaver turned and started walking back toward the pool and dam. The action astonished and baffled me. C'mon I said to myself! There is no way this water dwelling animal could possibly have understood what I was saying to it. Could it have? Did my experience in the Aspen grove somehow give me an enlightened ability to communicate with other species of animals? I did not know what to think and began walking again following the creek up into the mountains still bewildered by the encounter.

The further I followed the creek on the bank the less wide it was becoming. I began thinking that the origin and source of this creek could be found if I desired to continue to that point. I made it a goal and proceeded further into the mountains following the creek along the bank. I carried a water bottle in my hand and repeatedly drank from it to remove a constant dryness in my mouth and throat.

At a point where the creek was only three feet wide I came across a couple of large pine trees about a foot and a half in diameter. The trunk of one of the trees was rubbed and scarred seven to eight feet from the ground. As I made my way through and past them, I imagined the huge elk from the grove striking his antlers against the bark of this formidable sparring partner.

I continued to hike further into the mountain crevice and soon the creek was a trickle of water twelve inches wide. The steep mountains had been reduced to a height of no more than sixty feet above my present location. I was confidant that I was getting closer to the source of the creek. Rocks of many sizes littered the ground throughout the area making it difficult to navigate the rough surface. The challenging terrain restricted the speed of which I could move significantly. Getting ever so near I kept going – until finally there it was!

I removed my pack and sat on the ground next to the origin I had assigned myself to find. A small amount of water no thicker than a quarter of an inch was leaking out of the mountain crevice from under a shelf of rock. The soil of the mountain absorbed the moisture from the slow melting snows of the season. The water collected deep within the earth and when it reached a point of maximum saturation it exited at this most unassuming spot.

Looking down at the gulch below I marveled at how such a small constant trickle could become the wider body of water well known to a lot of people called Trikum Creek. I began to think that there were many parallels between this creek and the flow of information into all human societies. It begins at the point of origin and gains momentum as it travels downward. When it encounters resistance such as an obstruction or higher ground it gathers together becoming larger until it overpowers each individual blockage. The process is repeated over and over as the flow continues downward. Whether the information is true or untrue by the time it reaches bottom it is widely believed to be true. False or misleading information is like water. It can possess the same power and ability to erode.

I took another drink from the water bottle to wet an unrelenting dry mouth and throat. I had two water bottles with me and they were now both empty. I removed the cap from one of the bottles and held it in front of the water coming out of the ground filling it half way. I lifted it over my head letting the light of day shine through to inspect it. There was no cloudiness and this water was clearer than any I had seen before. I took a small amount to taste it. Tasted good and was cold! It was a fitting end to a unique personal achievement. I have now taken a drink directly from the source and origin of the creek.

I sat next to the trickle of water coming out of the mountain drinking the remaining half bottle. The sun had moved across the sky during the day and was now behind the top of one of the mountains surrounding me. Fully blanketed by shadow, the temperature in the valley was getting cooler. I knew the dirt road leading to Trikumwith Water Canyon was on the other side of the mountain I was currently sitting on. I began to think that perhaps I should climb the short remaining distance over the mountain and hike the dirt road back to camp. It would be a little further then returning back down the route I came up, but should it get dark there would be no obstacles to contend with. I made the decision to climb over the mountain and hike the dirt road back to camp.

I filled the two water bottles with fresh water straight from the mountain and put them in the backpack. Now loaded and ready to travel I decided to tackle the steep slope of about fifty feet on an angle to reduce the incline. Halfway into the climb the dryness quickly returned in both my mouth and throat. My legs began to feel stiff and a hungry like feeling entered my stomach. I completed the climb to the top and stood upon the apex of the mountain. There was a heightened awareness within allowing me to feel and hear that my heartbeat was elevated. I looked at the altimeter on my watch and from the grove when last checked I had climbed an additional 204 feet in altitude.

I took a drink of water and began to survey my position in relation to the main dirt road. When I located the road in the distance I realized it was at minimum about two miles away. I concluded a straight path approach would be best but the climb over another hill was ahead of me. After a short rest I descended into the valley on an angle to make the slope manageable on foot.

The valley was a dry tan color covered with waist high brush and native grasses. There were no trees to shade the ground from the sunlight in this one area of the mountainous terrain. The distance to the next hill was somewhat wide and I started to cross preparing myself for the coming climb. The stiffness I felt in both my legs had now spread into my arms as well. A feeling of hunger like emptiness within my stomach was gripping at my midsection. I continued to take drinks of water as I made my way through the valley in an attempt to keep the dryness from returning.

I arrived at the next hill and without delay proceeded to make the necessary climb over. Again I climbed the slope at an angle and reached the top quicker than the last. With my pulse racing, and breathing heavily after the climb, I decided to rest and gain visual on the remaining distance to the road.

I looked in the direction were the road should be and saw only the vast rolling hills of the landscape. The crest on which I now stood was not as high as the last thereby removing any sight of the main road. I took a few drinks of water in another attempt to subdue the dryness. The view from the hill was indeed something to behold. In every direction that I looked there was only natural design to be found and no signs of human constructions. It was yet another first for me. I was beginning to feel as if I had a renewed sense of direction within myself.

Chapter VII

A small bird flew by the tent door releasing me from the stare that kept me frozen while the events replayed in my mind. I closed my eyes for a few seconds allowing my head to lower slightly and sat listening to the sound of my own breathing. Less than a minute later I opened my eyes and lifted my head. There was a haze still clouding my vision as I focused on the watch and read three twenty-one p.m.

I felt thirsty and began to look around the inside of the tent for a bottle of water. After sifting through some of the items I located one and saw it was less than a quarter full. It was enough for now and I proceeded to take a drink. My throat felt sore when I swallowed the water. An involuntary bodily reaction to the discomfort had me feeling my throat with my hand. The front and sides of my neck were slightly swollen and numb to the touch.

In smaller amounts I continued to drink the remaining water in the bottle. I would need a lot more fluid to aid in my recovery and the supply needed to be replenished. The increased popularity of the canyon campground over the years encouraged the installation of a well in the center of the turnaround circle. All visitors to the area could access fresh water by using the manual pump handle. I must begin to test myself and see if it is possible to get on my feet and refill the water bottles.

I still felt the nausea but the dizziness was not present at this moment. My legs and arms felt very stiff like they have not been used for a long period of time. There was an aching feeling in the joints and muscles throughout my entire body. I came forward on both knees and hesitated to see if there would be any adverse effects to the vertical movement. First step was to put one knee up, foot planted in front, and both forearms on top of thigh. I again waited. I felt surprisingly well at this point so I continued to push myself to a now standing position.

It was a wavering stance and I moved my arms around to assist in maintaining balance. The decision to reduce the speed of change from horizontal to vertical appeared to be working in my favor. I returned to a kneeling position grabbing a water bottle with each hand and crawled forward through the tent door and again stood up outside.

I took small steps rounding the edge of the tent and began in the direction of the well located in the center of the circle. The stiffness in my legs caused instability forcing me to deviate slightly off course toward a tree. I made it to the tree about thirty feet from the tent and used it as a brace by leaning against it. The dizziness had returned and I gripped the tree with one arm around it to support myself. The cramp-like feeling was aching in my right calf area and the moving weight of my body brought a sharp pain from the tendons of both ankles. My stomach felt empty and had the appearance of being shrunken inward when I crossed my other arm in front of my waist against the shirt.

I paused for several moments holding the tree and then proceeded to cross the dirt road into the brown grassy area of the turnaround. Keeping as straight a line as could be managed I made my way to the pump handle. My arms were also stiff and without strength requiring the use of both to pump the handle that siphoned the water up the pipe to the surface. With considerable effort and taking longer than I had remembered a small rusty colored trickle began to exit the spout of the pump. I continued to pump the handle increasing the flow of water from the spout as the cause for the discoloration slowly decreased. Satisfied with the color of the water I filled one bottle a little over halfway and began to sip at it. After a few drinks I filled the other bottle and capped it. I drank the remaining water from the first bottle and refilled it. Given my present state of condition, deterioration in my capabilities was possible, so I focused only on returning to the tent and without delay began the walk back.

Slowly and in a stumbling fashion I made it across the grass area of the circle and began crossing the dirt road.

An uneasy feeling was swelling inside as I made it back to the tree. I hugged the tree as though it was a dear friend I have not seen in a long time. The walk agitated and multiplied the pain in my ankles and I was getting very queasy. My body rejected the water it was given and I began vomiting while still holding onto the tree. The process continued for several minutes until all contents and a little more had been removed from my stomach. I waited a few minutes longer before trying to move. I stumbled around past the front of the tent to a folding chair by the fire pit and sat down.

I felt relieved that the water bottles were filled and at my disposal. I had lost a lot of fluid through perspiration and needed to replace it. Many people would view a bout of vomiting as a condition that required sleep or rest. I perceived it as a good indicator that my body was continuing to fight and remove what it was that ailed it so. Most likely it would happen again but I needed the water and began to take small drinks from one of the bottles.

My eyes were locked in a trance like stare directed at the fire pit as I sat slouched in the chair with my legs and feet sprawled out in front of me. Nearly five minutes later the pain in my ankles was beginning to subside. The dizzy feeling was again fading and being replaced by the start of a headache. I took a few sips of water from one of the bottles I had set on the ground beside the chair. My eyes embraced the fire pit renewing their stare and a minute later I began to remember more.

Chapter VIII

Now at a lower elevation the foothills were blocking any view of the main road that led into the canyon. I sat down on top of the hill and took a drink of water. If I could not see the road, then I would let the road reveal itself to me. I did not think it would take long before the magic of the dirt road delivered the correct direction.

While I sat patiently waiting for the inevitable to occur, the wind began to sweep across the top of the hill more frequently prompting me to inspect the sky. There was a line of darker clouds barely visible over the mountain range approaching from the west. I estimated about an hour before the coming afternoon storm moved over my location. I looked back in the direction of the road and saw what I had been waiting for. A vehicle driving down the road had created a rising dust trail for me to follow. I stood up loaded my pack and began descending the hill in the direction of the dust.

My legs were stiff and the dryness continued to bother me as I made it to the bottom of the hill. I began walking the ravine between the foothills in the direction of the road. It was best to not expend the energy climbing over the hills and staying below the increasing afternoon breeze may help with the dry mouth. I followed the crevices winding through and past several of the foothills continually sipping the water as I went.

A rumble of thunder broke the silence around me and looking back I saw that the storm was quickly approaching. The foothill curved right and when it straightened I could see another dust trail in the distance indicating that the road was ahead about one mile. With only a couple more hills to pass through it began to sprinkle. The sprinkles of rain and the thunder increased more steadily as I continued on. As I came around a bend between the last two foothills the land opened wider and a grove of trees was flourishing on both sides of a small creek. This creek about two feet wide exited the hills on the other side of which I had been walking. The terrain ahead was seemingly flat and I could clearly see the road about half a mile away. The rain began falling harder as I sought shelter in the grove of trees.

The foliage on the trees would offer some protection but I had no doubt that I was going to get rained on. I went to the middle of the grove and squatted behind the largest trunk I could find to block the incoming wind. I placed my pack on the ground, removed a heavy vest from it, put it on and buttoned it closed. I thought about how odd it was that an Aspen grove would appear in front of me offering shelter at the same time the storm was arriving.

The wind came in fiercely and the gusts were blowing in excess of fifty miles an hour. The temperature was dropping significantly, and in some manner that eludes my capability of explanation, I felt the barometric pressure dropping as well. This was going to be a very powerful storm.

The wind gusts within the storm began bending the tops of the trees in an angle I had never seen without them breaking. I grabbed the tree harder as the wind tried to push me over backwards. Drops of rain propelled faster by the wind were hitting my exposed hands. It felt like hundreds of pins continually pricking at the same time. I removed a backpack strap from my vest pocket and wrapped it around my left forearm. Then around the tree to my right hand and wrapped my right arm a few times. This allowed for my hands to escape the painful rain drops behind the trunk of the tree.

The strongest gust of wind yet came into the grove and took me over sideways to the ground. The plastic adjusting buckle on the strap slid tightly down against my left arm scratching it as I fell over. I stayed close to the ground watching to see if a tree was going to break and possibly come down upon me.

The temperature had dropped a good twenty degrees and my clothing became increasingly wetter as the storm seemed to grow in strength. The wind was passing directly through my water soaked garments and I had begun to

shiver uncontrollably. I remembered the heightened awareness experience a little earlier and how all of my senses
were in some odd manner being amplified. I had experienced sub zero temperatures, nearing lows between twenty
to thirty degrees below on several occasions, but could not
recall ever feeling this cold until now.

Hunched low on my side behind the trunk of the tree I
held the strap awaiting the next fierce downdraft of wind
to descend into the grove. I felt something come into contact with both my lower back and leg behind me. Startled, I
turned and saw a deer lying on the ground beside me. Then
looking to my other side I saw another. Both animals were
positioned with their heads low to the ground facing my
feet. The one was small appearing to be a little over a year
in age and the other slightly larger perhaps about two years
old. It was possible they were siblings and I began to look
around for any adult deer. There were three adult doe lying
in the brush about ten feet behind. They too had their
heads low to the ground but were facing toward my location and watching dutifully. I was neither perplexed nor
concerned by the actions of the deer. Thus far I had spent
nearly an entire day encountering several animals whose
actions indicated something further than the widely ac-
cepted label of wildlife.

One after another the strong winds and heavy squalls
of rain came down over the hill and bullied the grove
while the deer and I were now abreast in the grass. A couple of unprotected smaller trees to my left at the edge of
the grove broke at the trunk a few feet from the ground.

All fell in the direction they were being pushed by the wind. Then the storm began to calm.

I lifted my head to look around and saw debris ripped from the trees by the battering winds scattered everywhere within the grove. I did not move so as not to alarm the youngsters on either side of myself as I surveyed the sky with my eyes. The wind had slowed and the falling rain was steady but considerably lighter. The sky was brightening and I could see that it was beginning to clear in the direction from which the storm came.

When the rain was near ending the two young deer stood up and left my side rejoining the three adults behind us. They moved as a group across a small field and disappeared from my sight behind a hill. Did the deer use me as a shield or did they recognize my shivering and came to my aid? this is a question that will remain without answer. I do however know that huddled together we survived a very damaging and dangerous storm sheltering ourselves among the Aspen.

As I stood up preparing my gear for travel the sunlight peered through the cloud cover and started to instantly warm the air. To the east the sky was dark and the heavy rainfall took the appearance of vertical gray colored streaks descending from cloud to ground as the storm continued to move away. To the west the sky was bluing and the sun was shining behind the fading thin clouds that trailed behind the storm.

I was completely soaked and thought it best to dry off while the day sun was still available. I headed to a hillside about a hundred feet from the grove where full sun would be unimpeded. I removed most of my clothing and laid it on the hill to dry and began to realize that something was not well within me.

The sleepiness was returning very quickly and the dryness of my throat and mouth was persisting. My legs and arms were becoming increasingly stiff and a cramping pain was plaguing my right calf. But it was an unsteady inebriated type of feeling and clouded vision that made definitive to me that there was a problem. The symptoms manifesting within my body were clearly surfacing but for reasons unknown I was not alarmed.

I took a seat on the hill and noted that the one bottle of water was three quarters gone while sipping from it. The estimated distance back to my campsite was about five and one third of a mile so I would need to ration the remainder of my drinking water. The time was three minutes after five-thirty affording a couple hours of good sunlight left to dry my things. I had time to take a short nap and decided to do so next to the clothes on the side of the hill. Lying on my back I fell asleep as the sunlight brought warmth to me.

Chapter IX

The wood I had readied in the fire pit was not used and looked as though it had just been stacked. Sitting in the chair was helping to aid my recovery as I took another drink of water. Thus far my body was not fighting the necessary fluid and I was beginning to feel immensely better. A growling noise came from my stomach and I remembered a box of trail mix bars in the truck I had brought with me. It was highly probable that my body would reject it, but I should try to eat something.

I took another drink of water and stood up in front of the chair. I felt my front pockets for my keys and did not feel them. Unsure of my balance I walked slowly around the chair and made my way to the tent. I stepped inside then began sifting through the items spread about and still could not find them. I stepped back outside the tent and tried to remember where they may be, but was unable to recall any memory of them. Perhaps the truck was un-locked and I began walking slowly toward it to check.

The pain in both my ankles was quickly returning as I approached the rear of the truck. The tailgate was down and I leaned on it in an attempt to reduce some of the body weight my ankles had been carrying. The small cooler I had packed with several beers and ice was still in the bed of the truck. I lifted the lid to see that they were all there and now sitting in a half full cooler of water. The ice had completely melted and the resulting water was very warm to the touch. The bottles had been submerged in the water long enough that the labels were loosened and starting to come off.

After resting a few minutes, I rounded the end of the truck toward the driver's side door and lifting the handle found it to be unlocked. I opened the door climbed in and sat on the seat. The dizziness was still with me but had reduced to a much more tolerable level. I unwrapped and began eating one of the trial mix bars while resting on the seat of the truck. The bar was dry and hurt my throat when I swallowed. I needed the water that I left by the chair to soften and wash it down. I grabbed the box of trial bars, shut the truck door, and without hurry made it back to a sitting position in the chair.

I finished consuming the first bar and immediately began to eat another washing the small bites down with water. The pain in my ankles felt very similar to a bout of tendonitis I suffered from as a teenager while participating in high school athletics. At that age I was very active and on my feet nearly nineteen hours a day. In addition to normal daily walking, I also ran several miles per day on very uneven rough surfaces. The overexertion inflamed the tissue that connects the muscle to bone causing many hours of painful discomfort. If the condition was caused by fatigue, and cured with rest, then it made sense why the pain subsided as I rested now.

The replenishing of lost fluids was most definitely assisting in reducing the symptoms of which I was experiencing. Thus far my body had rejected what I had provided it with only once. I had given to myself an explanation regarding the pain in my ankles but still did not have any recollection as to what had caused me to become so near the grave ill. After my eyes had been glued to the ground in front of the fire pit for several minutes, I began remembering more.

Chapter X

After waking from a short and needed nap on the hill, next to the laid out clothing, I sat up and began to look around. It was exceedingly quiet and the only movement to be seen came from an occasional small bird on a routine fly by. The main road leading into Trikumwith Water Canyon was visible in the distance about half a mile away. Dusk was nearing and I looked at my watch for the time. It was seven thirty-two. I had slept nearly two hours under the warm sunlight likely providing enough time for my belongings to somewhat dry off. I took a small swig of water and then began to feel the clothes checking to see how much they had dried. They were still a little damp on the underside but it was much better than the previously drenched condition they were in.

Given the late hour and length of distance I knew that it was not possible to make it back to the campsite before dark. I would be hiking under the night sky a good portion of the distance so I saw no need to hurry on my way. I sat for a short length of time on the side of the hill taking in the scenery and resting.

I checked my watch again for the time. It was now seven fifty-six p.m. and I stood up to prepare for the hike back to the campground. I put back on the clothing, readied the gear in the backpack, and started to hike toward the road through the field. While walking I continued to sip at the water bottle. Twenty or so minutes later I finally set foot upon the dirt road. The water bottle I had been drinking from was now empty so I removed my backpack and exchanged it with the full one. I put my pack back on and started afoot down the dirt road.

As I walked it grew darker and the stars shone brightly in the increasing night sky. I was not aware of the current stage of moon cycle, but thought how it would be helpful if some light were provided by it in the coming hours of the hike ahead. If the moon were to show itself in the sky it would not be visible over the steep mountain peaks until at least ten o'clock or later.

There were no vehicles traveling the road, and none were to be expected at this late hour. Persons needing supplies or on errands would have went to town and returned to their campsites already. I hiked for a couple hours alone on the road as the stiffness throughout my entire body seemed to increase with each step taken. The persistent dryness felt as if it had reached a point of nearly closing my throat. This made it hard to swallow even the smallest sips of water. I felt unsteady as if I was in an ine-briated condition and had begun fading in and out of a sober reality. Then at last the moon began to show itself over the steep tops of the mountains. The time was now ten twenty-four p.m.

After traveling about half the distance of the main road back to the canyon entrance I began to hear the sound of yelping mixed with an occasional howling ema-nating through the rolling hills. As I continued hiking the sound was becoming louder and drew nearer. There was no mistaking the sound of coyotes on the hunt and they were heading in my direction. I looked to my right in the direction of the noises surveying the landscape and clearly saw the silhouette of a coyote walking along the crest of a hill. The rest of the hungry pack followed a couple hun-dred yards behind their appointed lead dog.

I continued to trek down the dirt road towards the can-yon and the wild pack of dogs followed my movement. It began to appear as if they were strategizing their position atop the hills on my right. I had never heard or read an ac-count of coyotes attacking a human but now knew it was I they had been following. Canines that hunt in packs such as wolves and coyotes have a yet unexplained ability to sense a weakness or sickness in the animals they select to hunt. The increasing symptoms of an illness plaguing me may have attracted the hungry carnivores. I have now become their intended target of prey. My mind was well enough to recog-nize that I was in the midst of a dangerous situation and needed to take action to thwart any planned attack.

I slowed the pace of my walk and began to study the hills for the whereabouts and total number of coyotes in the hunting party. The light from a near full moon was bright and would aid in revealing the location of any moving creature in the night. Most likely it was the alpha leading the eight others that followed shortly behind. That makes a total of nine in this pack. I needed to replace any signs of weakness sensed by the animals with a demonstration of strength.

I made a quick right turn leaving the road and headed into the field toward the foothills. The plan was to divide the followers from the leader by positioning myself directly between them as swiftly as possible. I walked briskly but did not run. Puzzled by my sudden actions the animals stopped moving and remained still where they were. Less than two minutes later I was between them on the top of the hill. I began walking directly toward the lead dog and it let me come within forty or so feet of distance before responding.

The moonlight was bright and I clearly saw a widening of the front legs and lowering of the head. The snarling animal began growling and took a defensive stance. It was about thirty inches tall weighing between forty to fifty pounds covered with mange spots in the reddish tan colored coat of hair.

When I was a child I had learned that a cornered dog will defend itself if it had no place to run. However, this dog was not cornered and I did not yet know if it would choose to run or stand ground and fight. I readied myself for a possible fight by removing my knife from the belt sheath and proceeded steadily forward revealing no fear to the animal before me. Almost immediately the now isolated canine turned sideways and began to back away while growling and showing teeth. I persisted in moving slowly forward as it continued to back away never losing eye contact of my movements. The plan was working and distance was being gained between the pack and their leader.

After a hundred or so yards I turned quickly around and began walking directly toward the other eight. They too turned and began heading away from their leader and myself. Only fifty yards later, I spun around yet again and saw the single animal moving back in my direction. Once more I started toward it. This time I stuck to it and followed in every direction it was going. After an estimated half mile, I saw the lone animal running through a field on the other side of a foothill trying to catch the others that were fleeing in the opposite direction. There I stood for several minutes watching with my heart racing within. As the pack moved further away it became apparent that they had abandoned their pursuit and with a sigh of relief I relaxed my posturing.

The brazen steps I had undertaken to end the coyote's intentions had removed me from the road a good distance. My full attention was required to chase the pack of wild animals away and I paid no heed to the whereabouts of the main road. The excitement had increased the drunken type of feeling I was experiencing and I found it difficult to remember the direction from which the chase started. My mouth was dry and I took a sip from the water bottle swallowing hard while trying to decide the direction I should start walking in. The moon was quickly crossing the night sky and the light it provided would be helpful for only a few more hours. I made a decision and began to walk.

For nearly two hours I wandered around through the narrows and fields of the foothills under the light of the moon trying to locate the main road. My thoughts drifted in many directions about a variety of different things, but never once did I think about the importance of locating the road. When I finally stepped onto the main road I paused to take a drink and check the time. The moon was now behind the mountains and provided very little light. It came as no surprise to me that it was now eleven minutes past two in the morning. The distance remaining to my campsite was at least two to three miles as I began to again follow the main road back.

As I walked the stiff feeling throughout my entire body intensified and the cottony dryness in my mouth and throat could not be remedied with a constant sipping from the water bottle. In a dazed state and empty of all thought I made it back to the wooden sign designating the entrance to the canyon. My legs and feet were weary from the long walk as I decided to rest at the entrance for a few minutes. I removed the backpack and placed it on the ground then sat down next to it leaning back against one of the posts supporting the entrance sign.

Each sip of water was becoming harder and more painful to swallow. The lack of movement was allowing the muscles in both my legs to begin contracting and cramping. My equilibrium was being affected and I struggled just to maintain a seated position without falling over sideways. I knew that I was ill and it was getting worse with each passing hour. Any prolonged delay would greatly reduce my ability to complete the one and one half mile long hike down the campground road back to my campsite. With all that had transpired through the course of the day it was not until now that I was beginning to feel a bit of fear come into me. The fear that I felt was not due to whatever it is infecting and sickening me. I actually feared not being able to complete the long hike back.

The cramping continued as I stood determined to complete the hike back to my campsite. I walked around a little to loosen the muscles and looking at the watch saw that it was now two fifty-six in the morning. After lifting and putting the backpack on the remaining walk down the campground road into the canyon was now underway.

A couple hundred feet later I began to pass the first of many fully occupied camping areas. There were no lights to be seen at this early hour and only silence could be heard as I labored down the road. The cramping pain in my right calf continued making each step more difficult than the last. In a dizzy and dream like state I crossed the second bridge on the length of road.

Chapter XI

Focus began returning and I found myself staring at the ground directly in front of the fire pit. I lifted my head and looked around while sipping water from the bottle. Gentle afternoon breezes continued to sweep through the canyon as I sat slouched in the chair unable to remember anything further than the second bridge.

For about an hour I sat in the chair slowly drinking the water in an attempt to replenish the lost fluid my body desperately needed. During this period, I saw no unusual movement around me and then something captured from the corner of an eye prompted a need to look. I lifted my head slightly and concentrated on the area. Oh $^* is an understatement! If I had not been lifeless and still enough previously then certainly I am now. It was a bear! A brown bear weighing at least three hundred and sixty-five pounds had approached through the brush and was now standing on the bank across the creek about two hundred feet away.

Many thoughts came and went with such rapidity that before one was complete another began overlapping it. I was in an open area with no routes of escape or means to defend myself should this bear decide to approach. Remaining completely still I watched for many minutes in an attempt to decode the mood and intent of this highly unpredictable animal.

Having looked directly at me and lifting the head several times to take in bigger whiffs of air, confirmed that the bear knew exactly where I was. I reached slowly for the water bottle on the ground next to the chair lifting it into my lap and paused. Slowly I removed the cap and took a sip. After replacing the cap, I held it in my lap with both hands and again paused. The bear watched my slow motion actions as I tried mightily to do absolutely nothing to either startle or provoke it. The do not make any sudden moves staring match went on for nearly ten minutes between me and this master of the timberline. However, only several minutes in, the body language and demeanor of the bear brought a sense of calm easing any thoughts of threat I had regarding the encounter. It never tried to advance or change position. It simply remained steadfast on the creek bank where it had first appeared. I was the temporary visitor in this place negating any claim so it would not surprise me if the bear moved in a territorial manner. But it did not. It seemed as if this bear was acting as a steward or guardian of this land and had come only for the purpose of checking on me.

Guessing either bored or satisfied the bear gave one last nod and began to retreat away from the edge of the creek. It slowly walked through the brush heading toward a small grove of trees growing at the base of the steep canyon wall. It entered the grove and then vanished entirely from my sight among the Aspen.

Relief seems to ordinary a word to describe the feeling that rushed into me. For now, the encounter with this particular bear was over. I now knew there was at least one brown bear in this area and perhaps more. If another were to meander my way, it most likely will not behave exactly in the same manner as the last. My mind was dominated by this only thought and I began to strategize a course of actions needed to prepare for another unwanted stealthy appearance of such an animal.

Remaining seated in the chair, occasionally taking small drinks of water, I thought quietly to myself. At this moment I was still very weak and feeling too sick to even begin packing the entire campsite. Driving over two hours through the mountains was also not possible. I did not have enough strength in my feet and legs to simply push the pedals eliminating the ability to operate a vehicle. I looked at my watch. It was now five twenty-seven. The end of the day was quickly approaching and it would be dark in a couple of hours. There was only one thing I could do. I needed to somehow safely stay at least another night and regain the strength needed to operate the truck. A few minutes later I had created a plan of actions that must be completed for the rest of the evening.

The first task on my list was to replenish lost fluid and nourishment. I had to eat and continue drinking plenty of water. I stood up and began forcing myself to make the walk back to the pump handle well in the center of the turnaround. I refilled the two bottles with fresh water. The walk again agitated my ankles and increased the pain felt in my right calf. On the way back I stopped by the tree and again used it as a brace to rest. I still felt a bit nauseated but did not vomit this time. I took it as a step in the right direction regarding the healing process.

I had packed and brought with me a small bag of supplies in the event that fishing did not yield enough for a dinner meal. I made my way to the truck where the bag of supplies laid on the passenger floorboard. I dumped everything out onto the passenger seat and proceeded to repack the bag with only what was needed. Reducing the weight of the bag would make it easier to carry back to the fire pit. I slung the bag strap over my shoulder, and by ignoring the crippling pain piercing through both my feet and legs, made it back to a sitting position in front of the fire pit. I checked the time again. It was now six twenty-one. I was aware of my slow movements, but could not believe that such simple tasks took nearly an hour to complete. I lowered my head in disbelief and confusion. I still had no idea what it was that caused the illness and placed me in this position of doing nothing more than just trying to survive it.

After a brief rest the pain had reduced to a more tolerable level. I began trying to make myself something to eat.

I unzipped a side pocket on the bag to remove a lighter and found the truck keys inside as well. I had no memory of how they got there but was relieved to have finally found them. After putting the keys in my front pocket, I leaned forward into the fire-pit and began to ignite the stack of wood. A package of beans and rice that required only adding water should be easy for me to prepare. When the high flames had reduced I positioned a metal grill somewhat level over the fire on which to put the skillet. My appetite was a surprise. I had eaten most of the ten inch round skillet full of food. I sat in the chair watching the fire while sipping water for nearly half an hour.

The next task was to thoroughly clean up any remaining food sources that would attract uninvited scavengers to the area, specifically those larger than me. All wrappers and packaging went into the fire for disposal. After scraping all remaining food from the skillet into the fire I turned it over and placed it in the center directly over the flames. In a few hours the fire will destroy any food remnants and the scent of food as well. There were still some food items on the truck seat and also the box of trail bars next to the chair that needed to be dealt with as well. I looked at my watch and it was now a little after eight in the evening.

After collecting all items around the chair and putting them in the bag I made my way back to the truck. I left the bag on the tailgate and with a bottle in each hand began the painfully hard walk toward the pump handle yet again. It was not getting any easier and suffering came with every step taken. I began pumping the handle and immediately felt pain in my wrist, elbow and shoulder. Every joint of my body was causing discomfort and aching when used. The severe pain felt in my lower extremities multiplied when these joints bore the shifting weight of my body.

I filled both bottles and slowly made my way back to the truck. I packed all things food into the bag and hung it from a limb over the creek using a rope some previous visitor had the courtesy to leave for others. I had left one water bottle in the truck and with the other in hand returned to the seat by the fire pit. From here I would rest and ride out the remaining daylight.

With a fixed gaze I sat by the fire pit watching the flickering of the diminishing flames and listening for any sounds around me. It was extremely quite and still. I could hear the trickle of water flowing steadily in the creek sixty plus feet from where I was sitting. Then I heard a trout break the surface of the water in an attempt to capture an insect hovering several inches above. Based only on the sound I estimated the trout to be about eight inches in length. An occasional crackle came from what small amount of charred wood remained in the fire pit. My ability to hear was sharp and finely tuned to the surroundings of the area. I was able to separate the many layers of sounds and fully visualize one of my choosing. A thought came and with it an understanding. Any abnormal noises in this area are the result of my actions and movements. Having aroused curiosity, it was I who brought the bear to me.

I lifted my head away from the fire pit to look around. The flames of the fire were brighter than the sky and nearly a minute later my eyes had properly adjusted to the change. With the darkness of night swiftly approaching over the canyon it was time for the last of my planned tasks to be implemented. To safely sleep through the night, I had decided to spend it inside the truck.

The fire had now burned past the point of flames and a glowing pile of hot ash and coals were all that remained. The upside down skillet had settled and was half buried in the center of the gray ash. After surveying the area, I stood up and headed toward the tent toting the bottle with me. From the tent I removed the sleeping bag and zipped the fabric door shut. I made my way to the truck and opened the driver side door. I then tried to toss the bottle and sleeping bag across to the passenger seat. It was a weakened attempt and leaning inward to push the rest of the sleeping bag further across amplified the pain I was feeling. After struggling to get in I closed and locked the door.

There was an immediate greater sense of security sitting in the driver seat waiting for the sharp pains to slowly diminish. It took about ten minutes before attempting to make my way to the bench seat behind. Having never used the back seat for such a purpose I quickly discovered that it was a good foot too short for me to fully stretch out. Lying on my side with knees bent I settled in for the night.

For several hours I slept and then awoke. When awake, I checked the fire by looking out the back window, took a few drinks of water, and went back to sleep. Finally, a deeper sleep arrived and embraced me for the rest of the night.

Chapter XII

The sunlight poured into the truck cab as I began to stir and arise the following morning. I sat up and immediately looked out the back window in the direction of the tent and fire pit area. All appeared fine as it was left the night before. While looking about I continued to exit the deep slumber that held me captive for many hours. A quick glance at my watch revealed both the time and an improvement from the cloudy vision. It was twenty after nine in the morning. I made my way to the driver seat and reclined it slightly backward. It was beginning to get warm and somewhat stuffy in the truck and I rolled the window down allowing the fresh brisk morning air to enter.

The cramp-like pain in my right calf continued to draw my attention as I took a few sips from the bottle of water. With the painful feeling there was also an itchy sensation. Through the pant I began scratching the area and instantly caused a debilitating pain to shoot through my entire leg in all directions. I began to think that there was an injury and was not aware of it until now. The pant leg would not go high enough so I would have to get out of the truck and remove the pants to inspect my leg.

I sat in the truck taking drinks of water allowing myself to fully awaken for nearly a half an hour. I felt a lot better than the previous day but knew that further examination was needed. The day was still young and only by testing my body would I know the limits of my present capabilities. From the moment of first awakening I periodically eyed the surrounding areas of the campground. My confidence to exit the vehicle continued to grow each time a visual survey was done. A perception had changed and understanding came as I thought about it. The familiarity of the vehicle I used on a routine daily basis at home had now become a crutch of security in a sickened and weakened state.

After unlocking the door and opening it I put both feet on the ground and came to full stance while holding the inner armrest to balance myself. Without taking a single step I realized the pain in my legs and feet did not feel any different than the day before. I made my way to the rear of the truck and sat on the tailgate. After undoing my belt and pants, I worked them down past my rear to my ankles. With my feet dangling a few inches above the ground I began to inspect my right calf for any sign of visible injury.

It was by far one of the ugliest injuries I had ever seen. The entire calf was bruised and swollen. About two inches below the back of my knee on the inner top part of the calf muscle there was a golf ball sized area colored differently than the rest of the bruise. The dirty yellowish color of this area contrasted with the darker hues around it. I began remembering the sage bush I kneeled hard into while climbing out of the creek from fishing.

The color of this area indicated a high probability of infection and I began looking closer to see if a branch had created a puncture wound. There was nothing large and because the top layers of skin were dry and peeling in this area a small wound was nearly impossible to see. I leaned in closer and saw a tiny dot beneath the surface of dry flaking skin. The finding led me to believe that perhaps a cactus thorn hidden within the brush was the cause of the infection. The wound needed to be addressed and I planned to do so on the drive back into town.

The rest of the morning and early afternoon was spent in the chair near the fire pit. Occasionally I tested the pain level in my legs and feet by taking short walks only to learn that the healing process was yielding little to no result. I made a late lunch out of a can of soup from my bag of supplies. After eating I closely examined my watch and made a startling discovery. I arrived on Saturday – and it was now Wednesday. According to the date I had slept three days inside the tent and was now on the fifth day of what was supposed to be a weekend trip of only two days. This explained why the campground was completely empty and I was the only one left in it. Everyone else had packed up and left at the end of the holiday weekend.

The itchy sensation from my calf increased as I sat resting in the chair. Having caused myself unwanted pain I was not going to scratch it again. A thought came that moistening the area with water would likely remedy the itch and again I undid my pants and lowered them to my ankles. I poured water from the bottle over the area and after waiting several minutes repeated the process. The itching subsided with each pour. Again I inspected the wound closely and this time could not believe what I saw.

I sat fully back in the chair and let my head go backward hanging over the top to a point of looking straight up at the sky. I rolled my head from side to side in a gesture of no and disbelief. How could I have missed this! All that had transpired became clearer and was connected to this one thing I had somehow overlooked.

After moistening the surface of my calf with water I saw a very faint second dot less than an inch from the other. When my knee came down in the bush on the creek bank I paused for nearly fifteen seconds to regain my balance and reposition the gear on my shoulder. It was not the branches of the bush I felt poking at me. Hidden within the bush I kneeled upon was a snake and it had bitten my leg. The visible difference between the two dots indicated that one fang went deeper than the other suggesting an angled strike. Most likely full penetration was not achieved through my pants. However, it was enough to allow the poisonous venom of this creature to enter my body and cause the damage of which I had and am still suffering.

As I sat deeply in thought many of my questions were answered but a few still remained. It is a known fact that the venom from a poisonous snake can be deadly to any human being. I began to think that at some point during the three days I was on my back unconscious in the tent that either my heart or respiratory system had failed. With no knowledge or experience of such a thing I will never know if I had actually died and returned from it. I can only say that based on what small amount I remember it may indeed have happened. It was at this time that I first felt and realized something more than the known human senses.

Five days had elapsed and carried by the bloodstream the poison is undoubtedly everywhere in my body. Reaching a medical facility that has anti-venom is an issue and at this point it may offer little assistance. Having read some print on this subject I believed the worst was now over and had survived it. I always carried an expansive first aid kit in my backpack that included supplies to treat a bite from a snake. I made my way to the tent and after retrieving the first aid kit returned to sitting in the chair by the fire pit. Following the paperwork accompanying the snake bite supplies I tended to the wound, cleaned, and dressed it.

For several hours I continued to test myself with small tasks and short walks to the pump handle well. The pain was unrelenting and my strength diminished the more I exerted myself. By late afternoon the reality of having to remain yet another night had set in. It was the first full day I had ever spent consciously isolated from human society alone in the campground. An entire day had passed and never once did I see a plane passing over. I grew increasingly eager to leave but my body was not able to perform the needed functions to do so.

It took an additional two days of nursing to better my health before attempting to make the drive out of the mountains back into town. I had now been absent from home for a week and many close to me would surely have taken notice.

On the drive back home my mind was heavy with thought about the whole of experiences on that first day. I had begun to suffer the effect of the venom prior to what many would deem an unusual animal encounter. I came to believe that somehow these so called wild creatures sensed or detected the poison within me. Perhaps they simply acted to bring it to my attention. Any attempt to describe these events to another would likely be dismissed as hallucinations brought on by the effects of the toxin. I convinced myself that such things could not be explained to others without sounding a bit off. Fearing ridicule, I decided to never mention it and keep it all within.

Chapter XIII

It was during the first weeks of my recovery period when I began to recognize subtle but definite changes with myself. Still weakened and in a sickly condition there were many days when I would simply retreat to the comfortable safety offered by the backyard. I remember doing nothing more than just sitting for many hours each day under the shade of a tree.

Often I sat directly on the ground and leaned back against a tree of my choosing. It was middle summer and despite the sweltering heat bearing down upon me, I seldom recall ever having a beverage while sitting for as many as six to seven hours at a time. Never once did I think about if another had witnessed my doing this or what they may have perceived from it. Nor has anyone ever approached or inquired as to what it was I had experienced during these very lengthy meditative sessions. So what exactly did I experience?

As best I can recall, the first couple of times were spent staring blankly at a branch of a distant tree. I had absolutely no thoughts and never looked in any other direction. I sat motionless and the hours would pass as if they were only minutes until the dark of night would end that particular day. After several of these same engagements it all began to change. About four hours into one of these sitting spells my sight suddenly went blank.

This blackout was less than ten seconds long and was immediately followed by a series of extremely bright flashes spanning near a full minute in length. My gaze remained affixed to the branch which grew harder to see over the ever increasing brightness the eyes were now encountering.

A single picture of an article from a medical journal I had reviewed many years ago suddenly appeared in my mind. The information it contained was relevant to the extreme brightness in my vision. The articles findings were in regards to a decade long study of people who had actually died in the hospital and then returned to life. Many in the case study interviews had reported seeing or experiencing "bright lights" somewhere between life and death. The study focused primarily on either a restriction or complete loss of vessel flow to the eyes. Immediately I began to think – this is it. After all I have gone through and fighting for weeks with all my might to stay alive, it was now going to claim my last breath.

I did not move. I sat motionless and just continued to stare at the same branch on a tree in the distance. I was calm as ever, almost comatose. A thought, completely void of any emotional understanding, came from my brain. If I were to fade from life at this moment, there was no one around to revive me, so why worry?

There I remained sitting for several more hours. The extreme brightness was ongoing and revealed no indication of intent or remedy. Shining a one million candle power spotlight directly into your eyes at point blank range for hours is as close a description that can be offered for what I viewed at this time. I had no further thoughts and was completely uncaring of anything.

As a child of less than ten years my siblings and I would often interact and create games we could play together. Many of these games were challenges involving body parts like can you wiggle your ears? Or can you curl your tongue? On one such occasion we accidentally discovered a strange bodily reaction. With closed eyes we would press firmly down on them with our fingers. The pressure would eventually trigger a "bright light" sensation that we could clearly see through our closed eyelids.

When the day began to end it grew darker outside and the blinding brightness slowly faded returning my vision to a prior status of known normalcy. I did not view this day as complete despair or beyond hopelessness. It was in fact quite the opposite. The blackout and hours long blocked vision had ignited something deep within me and for the first time in nearly two weeks I actually formed a mental thought. This was the day of the imparting.

As I slept that night what can only be described as visions powered through my mind one after another. Dreams usually have an underlying theme or plot. Many include familiar faces or areas known to the dreamer. These did not. I had never before seen these people or places. They were like pictures or snapshots that came and left. None seemed to be either related or connected to each other in any manner. Nor was I able to recognize any chronological order.

The following day I again made my way into the back-yard and took a seat on the ground under a tree. The need to find and stare blankly at a single branch was not with me anymore. I willingly began to look around the yard in many different directions.

Information that had long ago been learned mixed with recently absorbed material began flowing freely through my mind. I spent several hours looking about the yard deep in thought covering a wide variety of different subject matter. Occasionally I would look to another area of the yard while still formulating complicated thought in my mind.

With my hands clasped together on my lap I looked down beside myself and focused on a single ant moving on the ground. For reasons unknown I was completely intrigued by this one ant. I watched intently for nearly an hour as the ant appeared to be randomly moving across the vegetation and soil surrounding the area. I began to wonder if it was scurrying about in an attempt to happen upon what we humans refer to as "road kill." Perhaps in the ant world the equivalent might be the carcass or re-mains of a recently perished fellow insect. If successful, the ant would then drag the find back to the colony. A colony is by all descriptive functions a working commune where all cater to the ruler and share equally. Could not help but think that this may possibly be how our human predecessors created a type of governing body.

Throughout history human beings have created a great many things now used in modern societies whose origin was directly derived from the vast insect population of our planet.

A Prime example would be the hexagon. The hexagon is a six-sided geometric shape. Every known honeybee colony creates this shape in their hive. The same geometric shape is created one onto another in an inter-locking pattern. The repeated building upon of the same six-sided shape grows larger in size within the hive. The cavity or interior of these six-sided building blocks used by the bee is from where the honey is produced. The entirety of this built system of connected hexagons is known as a honeycomb.

The same six-sided shape is now used in the modern chemical charts and graph system taught to children. My thoughts split in two directions as I began to question a timeline of which came first. Has the honeybee been creating this shape long before humans used it to represent a chemical connecting system? Or did a bee read about this shape and decided that all bees on the planet will use it in their hives? So I ask myself, "which came first the honeybee or the chemistry book?'

The binding of communism is usually held together by coercive strategy. The greatest of these strategies now dominating the globe is an invention by humans known as money. From the humble beginnings as a tool of trade for produced goods, money has evolved into a symbol of power, control, and used frequently to manipulate the actions of the masses. History has recorded that many humans have acted in poor judgment for no other reason than to gain money. Individuals with access to large audiences are most favored and commonly used. Oppressed desperate individuals can also be secretly paid by agents of the regime to covertly keep eyes on many others. All of these humans are used to promote, support, and convert primarily the young gullible mind. Perhaps the phrase "busy bee" was created to describe these purchased individuals.

Eventually I lost sight of the ant as it moved further and further away. The ant was gone but the trails it left in the loose top layer of dirt were still visible. The directions the ant had traveled were now drawn directly onto the earth. As I thought about it, this drawing can be used as a time saving shortcut. If one can recognize and knows what to look for the time spent watching the ant's path would not be necessary. This thought led to another and before long I found myself immersed in expanding thoughts regarding the lines that were now clearly drawn in the sand.

I spent the remainder of the day deep in thought as my mind took me from one end of the world to the other on a variety of different subjects. Mentally exhausted I retired for the evening. There were no flash visions this night and I slept well for many hours getting some much needed rest.

When I awoke there was a different feeling. A need to rush had persuaded me to quickly get up, head out back, and resume a stationary position from which I could think. I did not attempt to restrain myself and instead welcomed this feeling of ambition that has been absent me for quite some length of time.

After selecting a tree and taking a seat at the base I began the process of concentrating on my thoughts. The brain was in control and most definitely dictating the direction of all my thoughts. Sounds a bit odd to say but my head now appeared to have a mind within a mind. It did not take long before I was deep in thought and quickly recognized yet another alteration in my previous abilities.

I was accessing information from the deepest areas of my mind at un-describable speeds. Knowledge or factual information that had long been forgotten or deemed not important enough to remember was again available. Everything I had heard, seen, read, or experienced from the time of being a toddler to present was again there for my use.

There was a lot of information which came as no surprise. I had always been an avid reader with a hunger for more, but there was something else, and it was hidden very deep within my memories.

I was a very young child and vaguely remember the information as non-useful. At that age my only interests where snack time and learning to ride a bicycle. That may be why these pieces of information had been put aside and forgotten for so long. It was there, locked away all these years, and I had now begun the process of unlocking it from the annals of my mind.

What this information contained brought a dark feeling to me. As the contents of these ancient files ran unrestricted through my brain I began to question myself. How do I know these things? How do I know where this comes from? How can I read this? How do I know what that means? Mathematics, languages, structures, origins, symbols, history, sciences, mechanics, codes and coding methods were all being reviewed. It seemed as if every alleged secret of the ancient and modern world was somehow contained in my mind.

I began to get an unfamiliar sensation never before experienced that abruptly halted my thoughts. The ability to receive a message without communicating in person or by device is merely an attempt to best describe what was occurring. This feeling or sensation continued for about ten minutes. The very moment it ended I was compelled to turn my head and saw a car coming down the road. The car then slowed and began to pull into the driveway. A family member had decided to visit completely announced. This family member lives about ten driving minutes away. Is it only a coincidence that both equal lengths of time occurred simultaneously? Odd? – Yes! Spooky? – Oh yes!! Especially the first time! It has been elevated to an uncharted level given this extra sense that I now know is operating within me.

While conversing with this visiting family member I found myself doing things I have no memory of doing before. When this person spoke, I closely watched the contraction and movement in their facial muscles.

The breathing pattern, pulse, pupils, and body language were all used as prime focus points. These same indicators were also employed to gauge how it was they were receiving the words I returned. It became clear to me that I was using this conversation time to practice and improve several senses that can be used as one. I was honing an extremely keen sense of observation.

I continued to do much the same thing day after day for several more weeks. At some point I began to task myself with small physical activities around the yard on a daily basis. The plan was to start with easy or light duty projects and then slowly ease into heavier workloads when ready. This would rebuild my stamina and aid in the process of gaining needed strength back. While performing these appointed tasks I continued to think about what I had re-discovered hidden deep within my mind. The information weighed heavily upon my every thought, but at this point I had no idea how truly significant it was.

During this period of self-rehabilitation, I had re-learned an enormous amount by way of an unexplained reset that has somehow enhanced all of my human senses. I have also been made aware of new senses of which full understanding has yet to be tested. The time to move past the cradle of the backyard would come when I could confidently think and say aloud that "My mind is strong and the body is as equal". That time has now come.

Chapter XIV

The next several weeks were spent feverishly gathering more information. I had lots of books in the house at my disposal and began to read through them once more. I was searching for clues. Some small piece that could aid in deciphering this deep hidden information I had recently recalled from the darkest areas of my memory.

I obsessively poured over every type of book that was available. Fiction, non-fiction, science fiction, cookbooks, children's classics, dictionaries, and then, -- I found something. It was a picture of an ancient inscription printed in a book of world history. Somehow I knew and understood every symbol carved onto the piece depicted. I read the caption below and discovered what was written appeared to be completely misleading. I focused my research on this one area. I had only several books on ancient civilizations and began looking through every one of them for more artifact pictures. There were a few, and again the caption below did not seem to accurately describe what was in the picture. I needed more information. It was time to venture out.

I traveled from one book store to another and browsed through all the publications available on their shelves. Within a few days I had purchased from several stores nearly two dozen books with printed pictures from a variety of ancient civilizations. Armed with many new resource materials I sat down and began reviewing them.

For a week and a half I did nothing but bury myself in these books. I took many notes, performed lengthy math calculations, and closely reviewed these items with a magnifying glass. Even the smallest of details could lend sight into fully understanding what they truly meant. Every caption I read under these printed pictures did not seem to fit. I also found that in some cases the picture was either printed in the published book backwards or upside down. I had discovered something and began to naively feel as if these items had been improperly interpreted by others for many years.

To confirm my calculative notes and findings I needed one more thing. I made a special trip to the bookstore to see if it was available. I was surprised to find that they actually had a couple of choices on the shelf. I needed a book on hieroglyphs. I came home and immediately began to review it. What I saw again surprised me. Not only was I familiar with the symbols, but actually knew the origin from whence they were created. The book I purchased asserted that the symbols were used to represent words.

Knowing the origin from which these symbols were derived made it difficult for me to believe this book.

I continued my work on decoding the hieroglyphs, pictoglyphs, and carved artifacts for a couple more weeks. Many notes were taken on which explanation could be offered regarding the items carved on the relics. The math was checked and triple checked for accuracy. I was excited by my findings and became anxious to share them with others.

When enough data had been accumulated I began the process of reaching out via telephone. I placed calls to four different state universities and asked to speak with someone in the history department. I was met with stern resistance from two and the calls ended quickly. I learned from another that the ancient mound building, and pyramid building cultures of the Americas was being taught by a professor that came from a known communist country. This I found interesting. On the fourth try I spoke for nearly an hour with a woman who stated she had a degree in history. I offered some information of which she could find no dispute and sounded interested to hear more. I gave her my name and number, but she never called back.

Two weeks later I was speaking with my mother and told her that I was getting ready to go to the barbershop. I drove to the store where I have been getting my haircut for nearly twenty years. I walked in and approached the counter. A woman greeted me and called another name. A man with dark brown hair, mid-thirties, clean-cut looking, not in need of a haircut, sitting in a waiting chair stood up and approached the counter. He seemed very edgy and nervous. She asked for his name and number and he loudly replied – "Mark – 555-5555." She asked for another number and he replied "I don't like to be tracked by my number so I don't give it out." He then turned and quickly left the store. Anyone would find this behavior alarming, but the employees of the store made no comments or reacted in anyway. Their actions indicated that this was pre-planned and they had been instructed that it would occur when I arrived. It was an attempt to scare or un-nerve me. It did not. I calmly proceeded and got my haircut. Afterwards I again spoke with my mother and told her of my odd experience that just happened at the haircut store. She then stated to me that the number was a government information gathering number.

A razor sharp intuition had guided me through the staged theatrics that occurred in the hair store. When the woman from the university history department did not call back I began to feel that something not good was occurring.

This pre-planned event not only revealed who they were, it confirmed the feeling I had been having. It also revealed that someone is undoubtedly listening to my phone conversations. It is the only plausible explanation of how they knew where I would be and when. Besides the bookstore visits, which came before calling the universities, this was the first public outing I had during my recovery.

The obvious motive is to silence me. This group of humans does not want me to share with others what I know. If others knew, many created untruths would be exposed. The unraveling would end their use as a power and control tool. This is what they do not want. There are many secretive cults that desire both power and control over all other humans.

It begins with a small group of people who create a philosophy or belief system. This small group then recruits and converts others into their philosophy of beliefs. Those living under this philosophy or belief system also produce offspring. From the time of birth these humans are cultivated under this philosophy or belief as they grow to adulthood. The numbers steadily increase and it is called a cult. Many who have been trained from child to adult never consider if what they were taught is untruthful or even evil. When a large amount of humans accept untruth or evil as their way, the rulers of the cult begin to use and then discard them. Cult is the first four letters of both the words cultivate and the word culture.

Many now known past cults have taken extreme measures to acquire power and control. Those with a secret agenda have known for thousands of years that the largest resource on the planet is human beings. Millions of humans have been, or can be, indoctrinated and radicalized simply by creative use of mass propaganda. The greatest of all human evils is by way of lie to enslave another.

I had now unraveled the mystery of the deeply hidden information in my memories. Buried deep within my mind was the capability to understand and decode the origins of anything created by humans. In an excited attempt to share a further understanding of our human past, I had inadvertently exposed my abilities and sight. They know that I am one who sees all and carries within the universal knowledge of human creation. I have come to understand that the only significance to this knowledge is to those who hide the truth.

My memories of this had fully recovered and I do recall having to hide many times as a child. I played dumb as a diversion to not reveal what I knew and was capable of. I also remember knowing that if exposed I would never again have free will. I would be constantly harassed and my every move shadowed. When old enough, I would likely have been taken somewhere I did not want to be and forced to do things I did not want to do. It was a careless mistake after hiding all these years. Being persecuted because you are smart is not called freedom? I had freely lived less than half a full life and that was all now going to be tapped, wired, filtered, and altered.

It took nearly five months to recover at home before I returned to work on a daily basis. There have been a few occasions when a lingering pain or dizzy spell would drag my memory back to the campground in Trickumwith Water Canyon.

As was previously planned, I never did speak of the odd encounters with the animals. In the course of my life I have known or become acquainted with thousands of individuals. While I was recovering not one person inquired directly to me about why I had been gone so long.

Many times I have crossed paths with someone I knew and each had a very different account about my alleged mysterious disappearance. Every story swirling through the rumor mill seemed indecent to my person. A male friend of twenty plus years shared with me what he heard and had been repeating to others. He stated "that I was found sitting in an open field unshaven and naked." According to his rumor I had been there long enough to have grown a full beard and mustache.

When asked, I began to habitually reply that I went fishing and offered nothing further. Apparently my silence on the matter had created a void to which many opportunists then filled untruthfully. The damage of slander is nearly impossible to reverse. Those who launch false character attacks diminishing another should always caution themselves before doing so. Law has been adopted by many global societies to hold accountable those responsible for the damages they created.

I have continued to remain silent regarding the details about what was intended to be a normal weekend fishing trip. Ample time has been provided to fully examine the behavior of the animals I encountered and weigh it against the behavior of many humans I have since dealt with. The simple truth is not as grandiose as the untruth therefore many refuse to accept it when spoken. To deny truth and espouse untruth greatly diminishes that which makes us human, it is called civility. In this manner perhaps it is human beings that are the wildlife and the animals that live and roam freely in the mountains are elevated to a higher order.

With the experience came both gain and equal loss. From it I gained a new perspective on the frail balance of life and a greater appreciation that was not present prior. Forever lost was a confident narrow view that such a thing would not happen to me.

An abundance of knowledge had been acquired and the return balance was the loss of a naive illusion of which I had lived for tens of years. As if this experience were not test enough, I had also gained an un-wanted following of prying cult eyes whose intent is yet to be discovered. Because I know what they have done, and how they created it, my freedoms to private conversation and travel without being shadowed now appear to have been forever lost.

As these pages now end, the tangling with those who hide truth has begun to write another book in a true to life hair raising saga. These events will remain forever with me, and that which is most kept, took place amongst the Aspen.

∼ **And it begins** ∼